This book belongs to:

_____

_____

_____

First published 2016 by Walker Books Ltd
87 Vauxhall Walk, London SE11 5HJ

This edition published 2017

2 4 6 8 10 9 7 5 3 1

© 1990 – 2017 Lucy Cousins
Lucy Cousins font © 1990 – 2017 Lucy Cousins

The author/illustrator has asserted her moral rights

Illustrated in the style of Lucy Cousins by King Rollo Films Ltd

Maisy™. Maisy is a trademark of Walker Books Ltd, London

Printed in China

British Library Cataloguing in Publication Data:
a catalogue record for this book is
available from the British Library.

ISBN 978-1-4063-7105-5

www.walker.co.uk

# Maisy's Sports Day

Lucy Cousins

WALKER BOOKS
AND SUBSIDIARIES

LONDON • BOSTON • SYDNEY • AUCKLAND

Maisy and her friends are very excited. It's their sports day!

There's a blue team and a red team.

First, everyone does
their warm-ups.
They bend and stretch.

"Gather around," shouts Ostrich.
"The first race of the day is ...

the egg-and-spoon race!"
"**HOORAY!**" shouts
everybody.

It is very
tricky ...
The eggs are
**SO** wobbly!

"You can do it, Maisy!"

Tallulah keeps very calm and steady and wins the race! But where is Eddie?

Poor old Eddie ...
He dropped his egg!
"Don't worry," says Maisy.
"There are lots more
games to play."

There's the wheelbarrow race ...

the hula hoop ...

the sack
race ...

and the
three-
legged
race.

They all wear funny clothes for the get-dressed-up-silly race!

Cyril is the winner!

Then it's time for a rest.
"I'm having fun," says Charley.
"But I REALLY want to win."

After that they feel much better.

Then they play quoits.
Eddie holds his trunk very still.

It's the relay race! Maisy and Charley run as fast as they can.

When Maisy reaches Cyril, he will start running. Tallulah has to wait for Charley.

"Faster Charley, faster!"

Last of all, there's a tug of war.
They **HEAVE** and **PULL** . . .

Then, with one final tug from Eddie, his team wins.

Everyone falls down laughing!

The red team has won but everybody had lots of fun. Hooray!
"I can't wait for the next sports day!" says Charley.